For my burrow-companions: Charles, Ben,
and especially Alex, whose dauntless spirit sparked this tale – D.R.R.
For Holly Winter, with love – S.W.

First published in Great Britain and in the USA in 2006
by Frances Lincoln Children's Books, 4 Torriano Mews,
Torriano Avenue, London NW5 2RZ

www.franceslincoln.com

Distributed in the USA by Publishers Group West.

British Library Cataloguing in Publication Data
available on request

The illustrations for this book were done in watercolour.

Set in Caslon

ISBN 10: 1-84507-400-9
ISBN 13: 978-1-84507-400-5

Printed in China

1 3 5 7 9 8 6 4 2

Tulliver's Tunnel

Diana Reynolds Roome
Illustrated by Susan Winter

FRANCES LINCOLN CHILDREN'S BOOKS

Tulliver lived with his mother on the edge of a wood.
Their home was a cosy burrow, lined with moss.

He was a happy rabbit, except for one thing.
His mother made him wash his face twice a day –
once in the morning and once in the evening before bedtime.

"I hate washing my face!"
Tulliver shouted every morning,
as his mother handed him
a damp cloth.

"Why must I be clean?"
he whimpered every evening,
as his mother rubbed a little sponge
over his whiskers.

One morning, Tulliver decided
he'd had enough.
"I'm leaving home," he announced.
"I'm old enough to lead my own life."

"Where will you live?" his mother asked sadly.
Tulliver pointed to an enormous tree at the
other end of their field.
"Over there, by the big oak," he said.
"No hard feelings, but no clean faces either!"
And he kissed his mother goodbye.

So Tulliver bounded over to the other side of the field.
He felt as free as thistledown.

On the way he bumped into a young squirrel.

"Where are you going?" asked the squirrel.

"I'm going to find a new place to live," Tulliver replied.

"Come and climb my tree," said the squirrel.

"There are beech nuts growing in it. We could have a feast."

"I'm busy today," said Tulliver. "I'll try your beech nuts tomorrow."

Halfway across the field, Tulliver met
a group of young rabbits who asked him
to play hide-and-seek with them.

Then he saw a butterfly, and couldn't resist a chase.
By the time Tulliver reached the big oak on the other side
of the field, the sun was already high overhead.

Tulliver started to dig
with his strong hind legs.
He dug and burrowed
and tunnelled, throwing
earth up in the air.

The earth landed in a heap, and the heap got bigger and bigger.

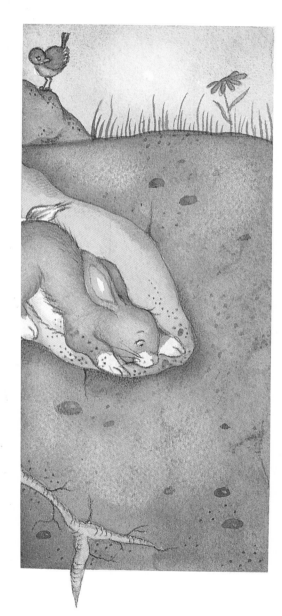 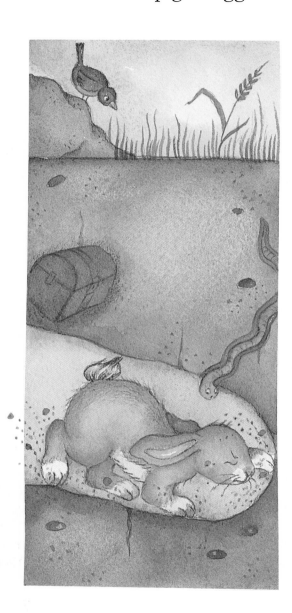 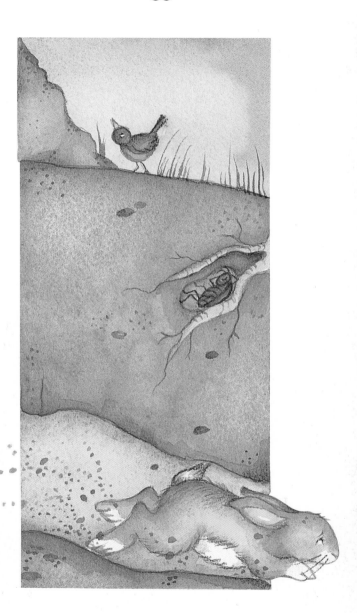

By lunchtime, Tulliver's tunnel was already deep beneath the field.

By mid afternoon, he was getting tired.
When he peeped out for a breath of air,
he could see his mother sitting under their beech tree.
She looked far away and a little bit lonely
at the other end of the field.

By suppertime, Tulliver was feeling very hungry.
As he sat thinking about all the things
he would like to eat, a badger's head
popped out of the ground.

"Don't let your tunnel run into mine,"
he said crossly. "You're getting too close for my liking.
Keep your burrowing to yourself, please."

Tulliver went down the tunnel
and started digging the other way.
He didn't want to bump into
a bad-tempered badger in the dark.

By night time Tulliver was feeling very sorry for himself.

His fur was muddy from hours of digging.

Tulliver looked at the pile of earth he had made.

It was enormous. He'd worked all day,

yet he still hadn't found a place that felt like home.

Tulliver's paws were sore and his teeth ached
from chewing through roots that had got
in his way. He would have to sleep
in the tunnel, just as it was.

He crept back into his tunnel
and lay down on the earth floor.

Tulliver thought he smelled
the faint, sweet smell of parsnips.

Then he fell fast asleep.

In the morning, he woke up
feeling much better. He seemed
to be in a big, airy den.

There was a delicious smell
of fresh cow-parsley. He opened
his eyes and there was his mother,
busy getting breakfast.

Tulliver had tunnelled right back into his own burrow!

"Welcome home!" said his mother cheerily, giving him a hug.
"I see you have your own front door now."

"What's for breakfast?" he asked. "I'm starving."

"Cow-parsley and carrots," said his mother.

"But Tulliver, you're muddy! No breakfast until you're washed."

Tulliver looked down at his paws. They were covered with mud from all that digging. Out of the corner of his eye, he caught sight of one dirty whisker.

"Yes, mother," said Tulliver, and he went off to wash his face and paws in a few drops of morning dew.

Eating his scrumptious breakfast,
he decided it was well worth a few clean whiskers.
Tulliver was glad to be home.

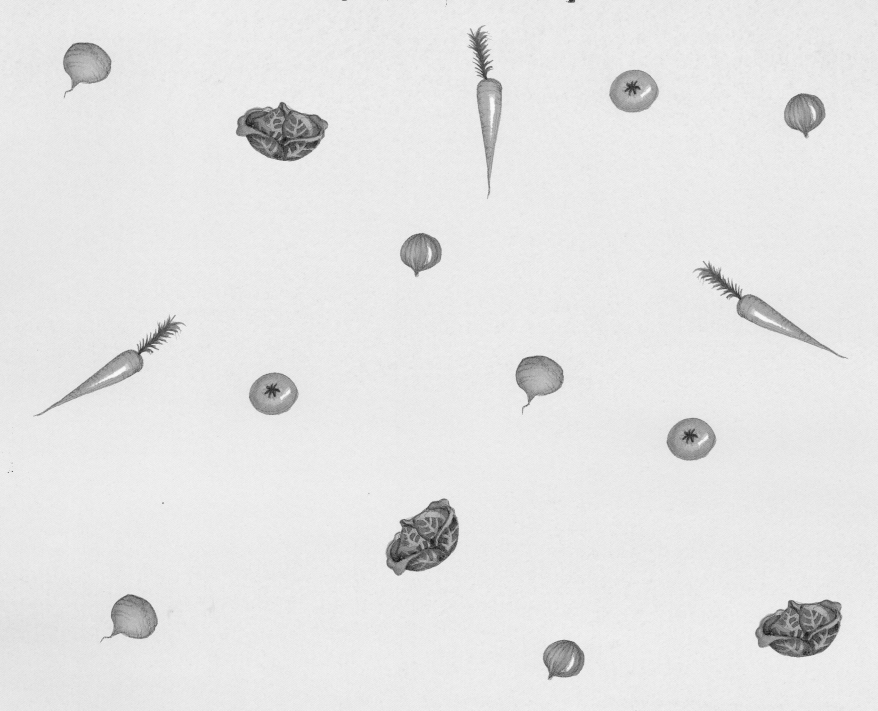